Sue Mayfield Rochelle Padua

I Can,

You Can,

Toucan!

Green Bananas

Crabtree Publishing Company
www.crabtreebooks.com

PMB 16A, 350 Fifth Avenue,
Suite 3308,
New York, NY 10118

616 Welland Avenue,
St. Catharines, Ontario
Canada, L2M 5V6

Mayfield, Sue.
    I can, you can, Toucan! / written by Sue Mayfield ; illustrated by Rochelle Padua.
        p. cm. -- (Green bananas)
    Summary: Best friends Toucan, Giraffe, and Penguin each dislikes something
about him- or herself, but when one of them is in trouble, it is their differences that
allow them to help one another.
    ISBN-13: 978-0-7787-1032-5 (rlb) -- ISBN-10: 0-7787-1032-7 (rlb)
    ISBN-13: 978-0-7787-1048-6 (pbk) -- ISBN-10: 0-7787-1048-3 (pbk)
    [1. Individuality--Fiction. 2. Best friends--Fiction. 3.
Friendship--Fiction. 4. Toucans--Fiction. 5. Giraffe--Fiction. 6.
Penguins--Fiction.]   I. Padua, Rochelle, ill. II. Title. III. Series.
    PZ7.M4676Iaab 2006
    [E]--dc22

                                                        2005035767

                                            LC

Published by Crabtree Publishing in 2006
First published in 2005 by Egmont Books Ltd.
Text copyright © Sue Mayfield 2005
Illustrations copyright © Rochelle Padua 2005
The Author and Illustrator have asserted their moral rights.
Paperback ISBN 0-7787-1048-3
Reinforced Hardcover Binding ISBN 0-7787-1032-7

Too Tall

I Can't Fly

Big Yellow Beak

For

George

S.M.

For
Sharon (aka The Other Dodgy Person)
Wojciech
The Paduas
. . . and Ebony.
R.P.

Too Tall

Giraffe is very tall.

When Giraffe plays in the park with Penguin and Toucan he bangs his head on the swings.

"You're too tall!" says Penguin.

When Giraffe goes for lunch at
Toucan's house he is too tall to
get in the door.

"You're too tall," says Toucan.

When Giraffe goes to the theater nobody can see past his head! "You're too tall!" say the people behind him.

Giraffe is sad. "I'm too tall," he says.

One day Penguin decides to fly her
kite. The wind is very strong. It blows
Penguin's kite up into a tree.

Penguin can't reach her kite. She tries to jump but she is too small.

She tries to climb

but she falls down.

"Help!" says Penguin.

Toucan tries to fly up to the tree.

But the wind is too strong.

He can't fly high enough.

"Help!" says Toucan.

"I can do it!" says Giraffe.

Giraffe stretches up tall

into the tree.

He can reach

Penguin's kite easily.

He brings it down again.

"Thank you, Giraffe," says Penguin.

"I'm glad you're so tall!"

"Hooray for Giraffe!" says Toucan.

I Can't Fly

Toucan likes to fly. He flies up in the sky. He flies higher than Giraffe's head.

You're higher than me!

"Look at me!" says Toucan.

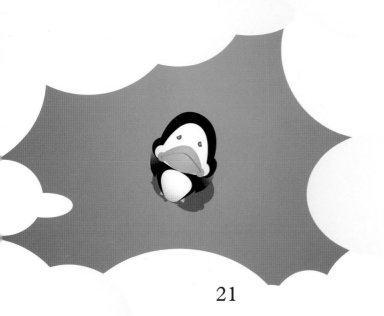

Penguin wants to fly too. "I wish

I could fly like Toucan," she says.

Penguin tries to fly.

She stands on a chair and *jumps off.*

Bump!

Penguin lands with a
crash.

Ow!

"I can't fly," she says sadly.

"Try again," says Toucan.

So Penguin tries running fast.

"Faster! Faster!" says Giraffe.

But Penguin still can't fly.

24

Penguin tries flapping her wings.

"Flap them harder," says Toucan.

But Penguin's wings aren't big

enough. She still can't fly.

Penguin is sad. So the friends play

soccer to cheer her up.

But Giraffe

kicks

the ball too hard . . .

27

. . . and it lands in the river.

"Oops!" says Toucan.

"Help!" says Giraffe. "I can't swim."

"I can swim!" says Penguin. She

jumps into the water.

Penguin can swim very fast. She can even swim underwater like a fish. In no time at all she brings the soccer ball back to Giraffe and Toucan.

"Hooray!" they say. "We're glad

you can swim, Penguin!"

Big Yellow Beak

Toucan's beak is big and yellow.

Bright yellow.

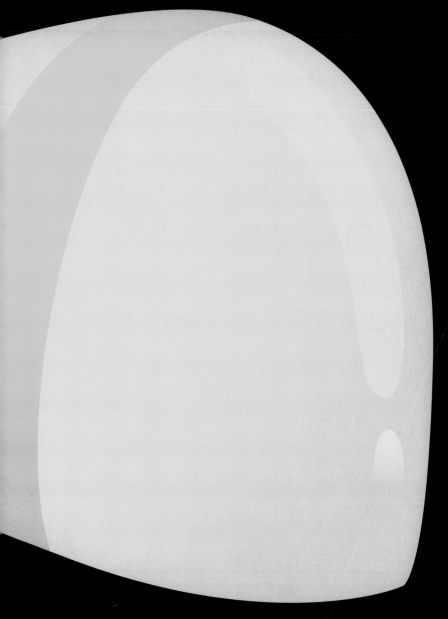

Other birds laugh at
Toucan's beak.
"Banana beak!" they
call him.

"Don't listen to them," says Penguin.

But Toucan is sad.

"I wish my beak was gray or black

like other birds," he says.

I like your beak!

"Come for a walk with us, Toucan," says Giraffe. But Toucan doesn't want to.

"People will see me and laugh," he says.

So Giraffe and Penguin go

for a walk without Toucan.

Giraffe and Penguin walk

a long way.

They walk so far that they get lost.

It starts to get dark.

Penguin and Giraffe are frightened.

"Help!" they say.

where are they?

Giraffe and Penguin
have been gone a long
time. Toucan is worried.

So he goes to look for them. He flies

a long way through the dark night.

Suddenly, Giraffe spots Toucan's bright yellow beak.

"Look!" he says. "It's Toucan!"

Toucan's beak is very bright. His friends can see it even in the dark! Toucan flies in front of Giraffe and Penguin.

"Follow my beak!" says Toucan.

"I can lead you home."

Thank you!

"Thank you, Toucan," says Penguin.

"Hooray for Toucan's big yellow

beak!" says Giraffe.